Turtle Bay

SAVIOUR PIROTTA

Pictures by NILESH MISTRY

FARRAR, STRAUS AND GIROUX   NEW YORK

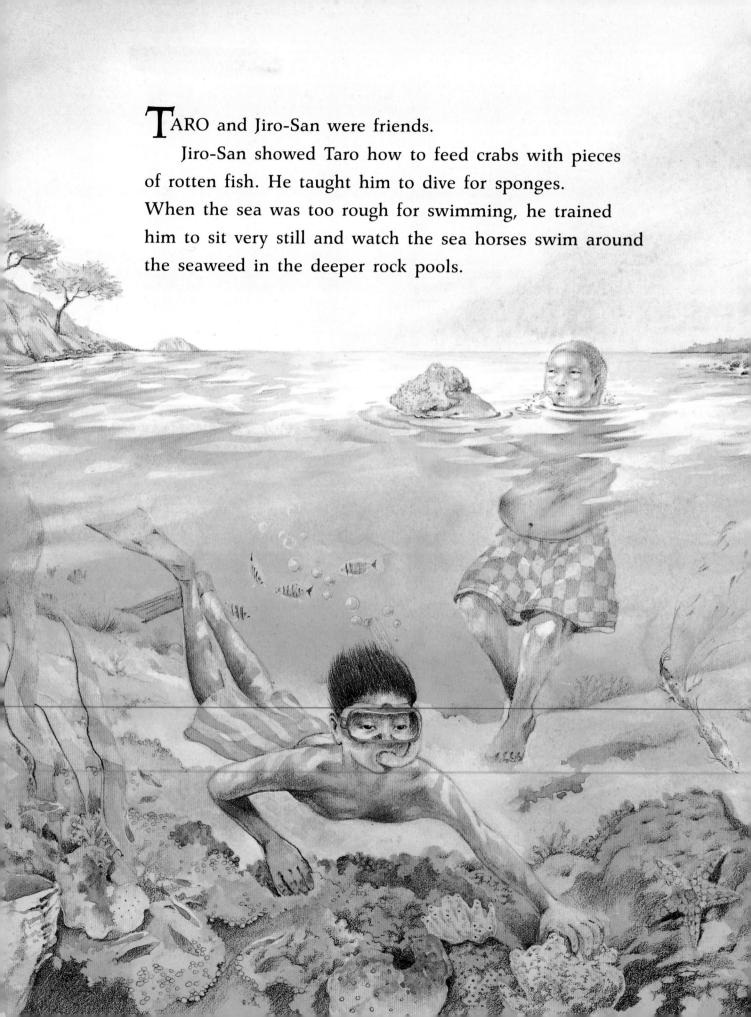

TARO and Jiro-San were friends.

Jiro-San showed Taro how to feed crabs with pieces of rotten fish. He taught him to dive for sponges. When the sea was too rough for swimming, he trained him to sit very still and watch the sea horses swim around the seaweed in the deeper rock pools.

Taro's sister, Yuko, didn't like Jiro-San.
"He's weird," she said. "Last year my friends
saw him sweeping the beach with a broom."
"No, he's not," said Taro. "He's old and wise,
and full of wonderful secrets."

One day, Taro found Jiro-San sitting on a big rock.

"What are you doing?" he asked.

"I am listening," said Jiro-San. "The wind is bringing me a message." Taro sat on the rock and listened. But all he could hear was the seagulls crying.

"Ah," said Jiro-San at last. "Now I understand... My old friends are coming."

"Who are your old friends?" asked Taro.

"You'll see," said Jiro-San.

Next day, Jiro-San brought two brooms and handed one to Taro.

"For sweeping the beach," he said.

Taro's heart sank. Yuko was right after all—Jiro-San was weird.

"There's a lot of rubbish and broken glass on the beach," Jiro-San explained. "My friends won't come if there is broken glass. They know they'll get hurt."

The boy and the old man swept the beach from one end to the other. They collected all the rubbish and put it in Jiro-San's cart. Soon the beach was cleaner than it had been all summer.

Jiro-San looked pleased.

"Meet me by the big rock tonight," he told Taro.

Taro ate his supper as fast as he could.

"You seem in a big hurry," said his mother.

"I am," said Taro. "Jiro-San's old friends are coming."

"Who are they?" his mother wanted to know.

"It's a secret," said Taro.

"What kind of secret?" Yuko asked.

Taro didn't answer. He washed his hands and went out to find Jiro-San.

"Look," said the old man, pointing out to sea.
Taro saw a school of dolphins riding the waves.
"Are they your old friends?" he asked.
"No," said Jiro-San. "Perhaps they will come tomorrow night."

Taro waited patiently all the next day. In the evening, he met Jiro-San again. This time, the old man had brought his boat out of the shed. Jiro-San picked up the oars, and they pushed out to sea.

After a while, the old man said, "We've got company." Taro watched as a huge whale flicked her tail up out of the water. She had a calf swimming beside her.

"Are they your old friends?" Taro asked.

"They're friends," said Jiro-San, "but not the old friends I meant. Maybe they will come tomorrow."

The next evening, Jiro-San was in his boat again.

"Where are we going?" Taro wanted to know.

"Over there," said Jiro-San. He rowed out to a secret cove on a little island. There Taro saw three large fish with swords for snouts.

"Are they your old friends?" Taro asked.

"All fish are my friends," said Jiro-San. "But these aren't my old friends. They seem to be late this year. Perhaps they are not coming at all."

"Don't be sad," Taro said. "Perhaps they'll get here tomorrow."

"Do you want to come and wait for Jiro-San's old friends?" Taro asked Yuko after supper the next day. Yuko wasn't doing anything, so she followed Taro to the big rocks, kicking the sand as she walked.

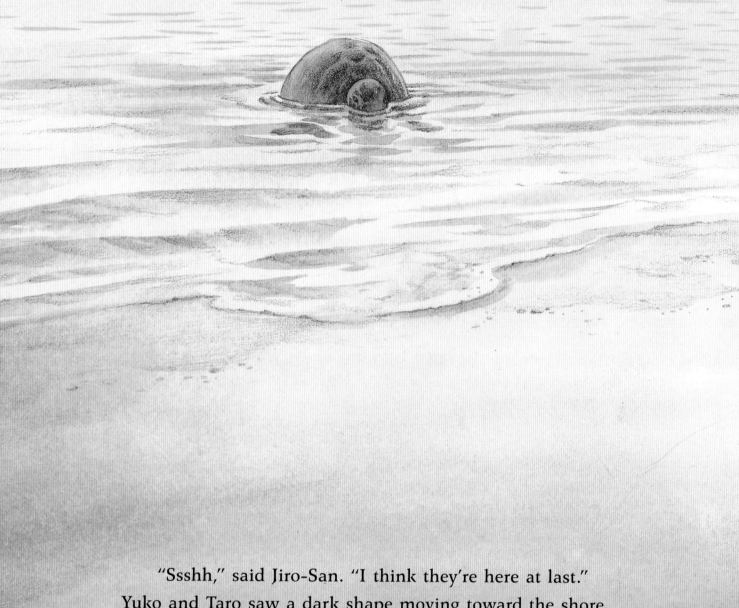

"Ssshh," said Jiro-San. "I think they're here at last."
Yuko and Taro saw a dark shape moving toward the shore.
It was huge and bobbed up and down on the water like an
enormous cork.

At last, the children could see what it was—a turtle!
"She's coming to lay her eggs on our beach,"
said Jiro-San proudly.

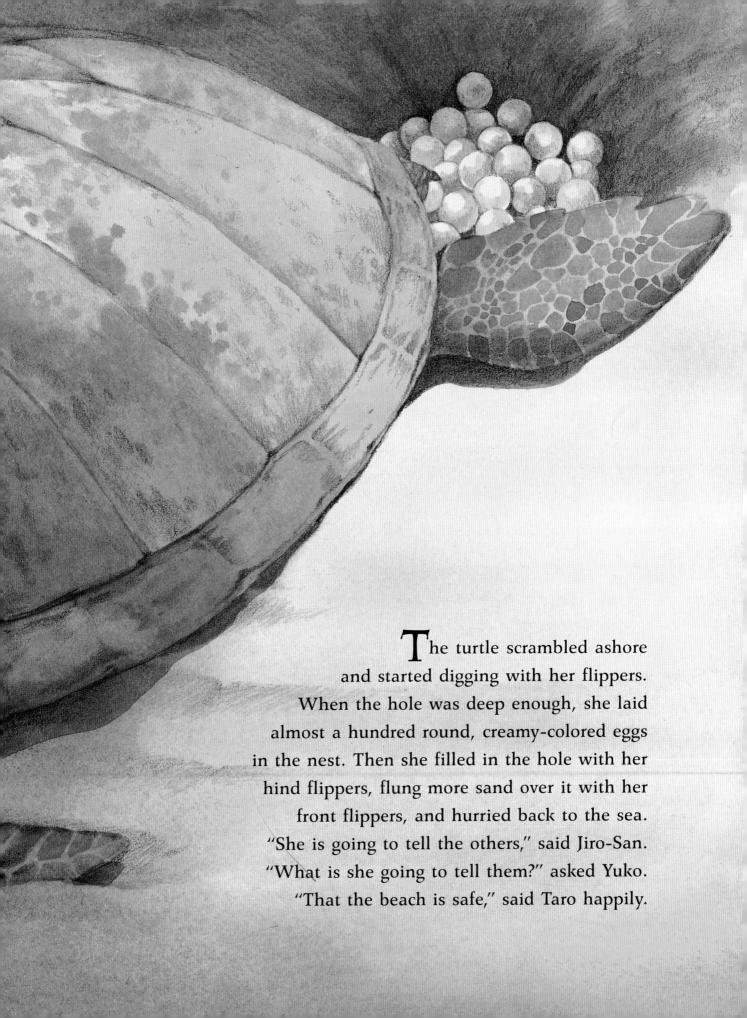

The turtle scrambled ashore
and started digging with her flippers.
When the hole was deep enough, she laid
almost a hundred round, creamy-colored eggs
in the nest. Then she filled in the hole with her
hind flippers, flung more sand over it with her
front flippers, and hurried back to the sea.
"She is going to tell the others," said Jiro-San.
"What is she going to tell them?" asked Yuko.
"That the beach is safe," said Taro happily.

The next day, Yuko came to the beach with her own broom.

"Can I help sweep the sand?" she asked.

"Of course," said Jiro-San. "The more of us there are, the safer the beach will be for the turtles."

The three friends swept up all the litter dropped by the beachgoers during the day. Then they sat on the rocks and watched more turtles coming ashore. There were lots of them, all huge and old and wise—just like Jiro-San.

"Now," said Jiro-San, "you must be patient, and wait until you hear from me again."

Eight weeks later, Jiro-San told the children to meet him at dusk.

"Sit on the rocks, please," he said, "and watch the ground."

The children looked and waited for what seemed like hours. As the moon rose, they saw something moving under the sand— something small and fast and eager.

"It's a baby turtle!" cried Taro. "The eggs have hatched!"

Soon the beach was full of baby turtles. There were
hundreds of them, all scuttling down to the sea.
The children couldn't believe their eyes.